I Love You So...

by
Marianne Richmond

sourcebooks
jabberwocky

I Love You So...

LCCN 2004115278

Published by Sourcebooks Jabberwocky,
an imprint of Sourcebooks, Inc.
P.O. Box 4410
Naperville, IL 60567–4410
(630) 961–3900
www.sourcebooks.com

Illustrations by Marianne Richmond

Book design by Sara Dare Biscan

Source of Production: Leo Paper Group, Heshan City,
Guangdong Province, China
Date of Production: November 2010
Run Number: 13876

Printed and bound in China
LEO 10 9 8 7 6 5 4 3 2

Also available from author & illustrator
Marianne Richmond:

The Gift of an Angel
The Gift of a Memory
Hooray for You!
The Gifts of Being Grand
Dear Daughter
Dear Son
Dear Mom
Dear Granddaughter
Dear Grandson
My Shoes Take Me Where I Want to Go
Fish Kisses and Gorilla Hugs
Happy Birthday to You!
I Love You so Much...
I Wished for You, an adoption story
You are my Wish come True
Big Brother
Big Sister

Beginner Boards for the youngest child
Simply Said... and *Smartly Said...* mini books
for all occasions

I Love You So...

is dedicated to

Cole James, Adam Jon, Julia Rose, and Will David,
who fill my heart with gigantic love. — MR

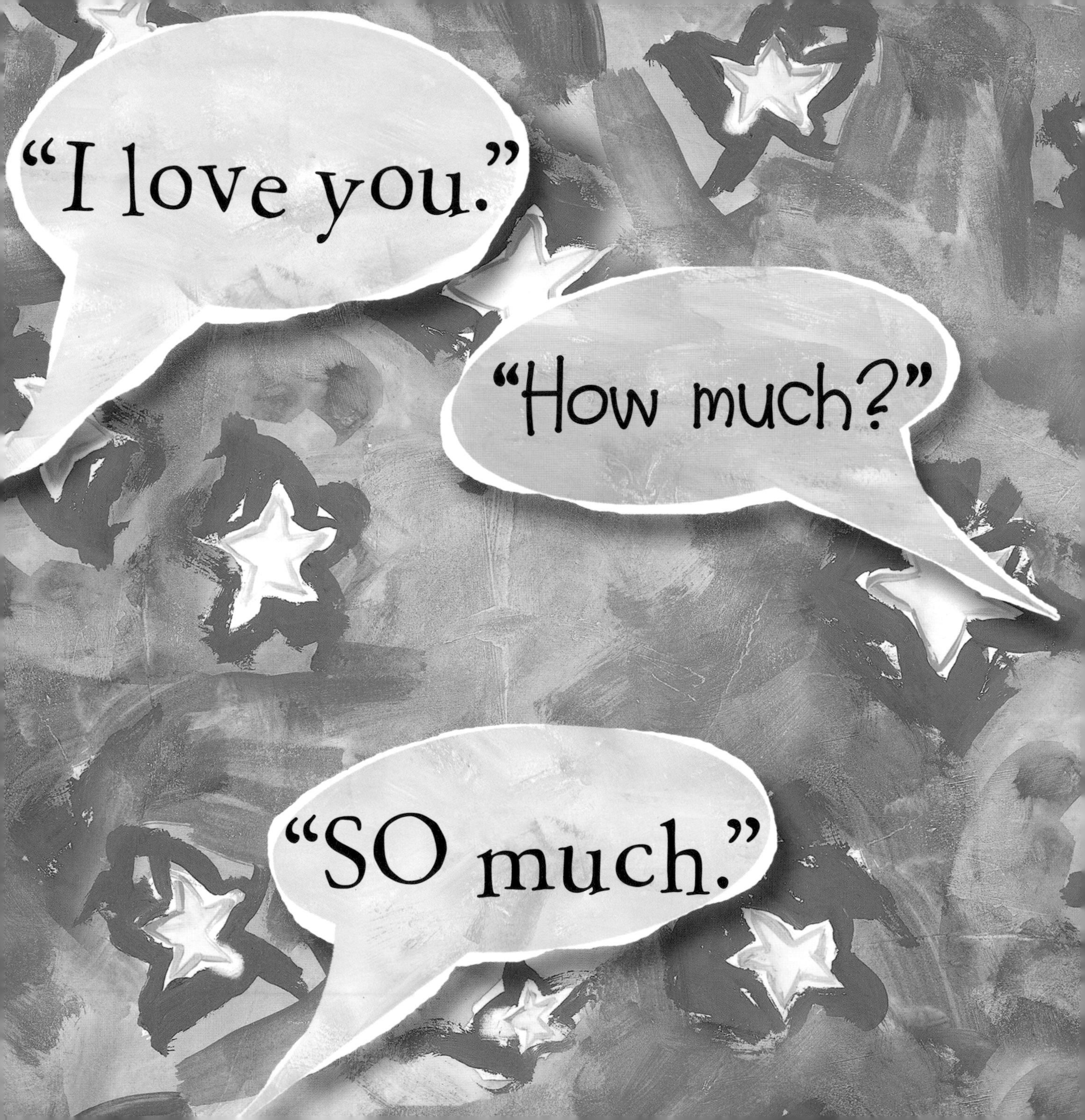
"I love you."
"How much?"
"SO much."

"How much is 'so'?"

"WAY, WAY MORE than you know..."

I love you as BRILLIANT
as each sparkling star,
and as WAY OUT as space,
I love you THAT far.

Marshmallows

I love you as GIGANTIC
as a great lion's roar,
and as DEEP as the ocean,
I love you MUCH more.

Don't feed
the lions!

"That IS a lot," you say,
"but HOW did it start?
WHERE did love come from
to be in your heart?"

YOU put it there, really,
when you and I met.
And I knew for certain
WITHOUT you I'd fret.

From MY HEAD to my TOES,
I was feeling inside
a devotion for you
SO DEEP and SO WIDE.

And now it's ENORMOUS
and wonderfully real
and hard to describe
HOW MUCH I feel!

I love you as AWESOME
as a thundery sky,
and as SOARING as mountains,
I love you THAT high.

I love you as SILLY
as a puppy dog's kiss,
and as QUIET as midnight,
I love you like THIS.

"Do you love me EVERY day?"
you ask with doubting awe,
"or does love go UP 'N DOWN
like a teetering see—saw?"

I love you as STEADY
    as the earth rounds the sun,
though SOME days of life
    are the FARTHEST from fun.

"Like when you feel MAD?"
     you ask with distress,
"'cause I've BROKEN the rules
     or made a BIG mess?

Or, when I'm UNKIND,
     and your feelings are BLUE,
do you love me ALTHOUGH
     I do what I do?"

I love you being NICE,
 and when you're CRANKY, too.
I love you without liking
 the NAUGHTY things you do.

My 'love you' DOESN'T change like the temper of the days. It's a CERTAIN kind of thing in many DIFFERENT ways.

You're my SWEETIE, my dear,
my SMILE and laughter.

You're my PLAYMATE for always,
and my JOY ever after.

Hanging out WITH YOU
is where I want to be...
eating ice cream sundaes
or watching the TV.

UNDER your umbrella,
  behind you on a bike.
BY you and BESIDE you
  is what I REALLY like.

"Do you love me just AS MUCH
when I'm FAR away from home?
Is your loving still THE SAME
in distant lands I roam?"

I love you NEAR or FAR.
I love you HIGH or LOW.
My love is there with you
WHEREVER you may go.

"Even when I'm SICK...
    and I can't get out of bed?
Do you love me better HEALTHY
    than with fever in my head?"

I love you sick or able.
    You're ALWAYS you to me,
the ONE I LOVE forevermore.
    Undeniably.

I CAN'T IMAGINE life
before YOU came along...
me there singing senseless,
no MEANING to my song.

Call it MEANT TO BE
or simply blessed fate,
you fill my heart WITH LOVE...
and for THAT I celebrate.

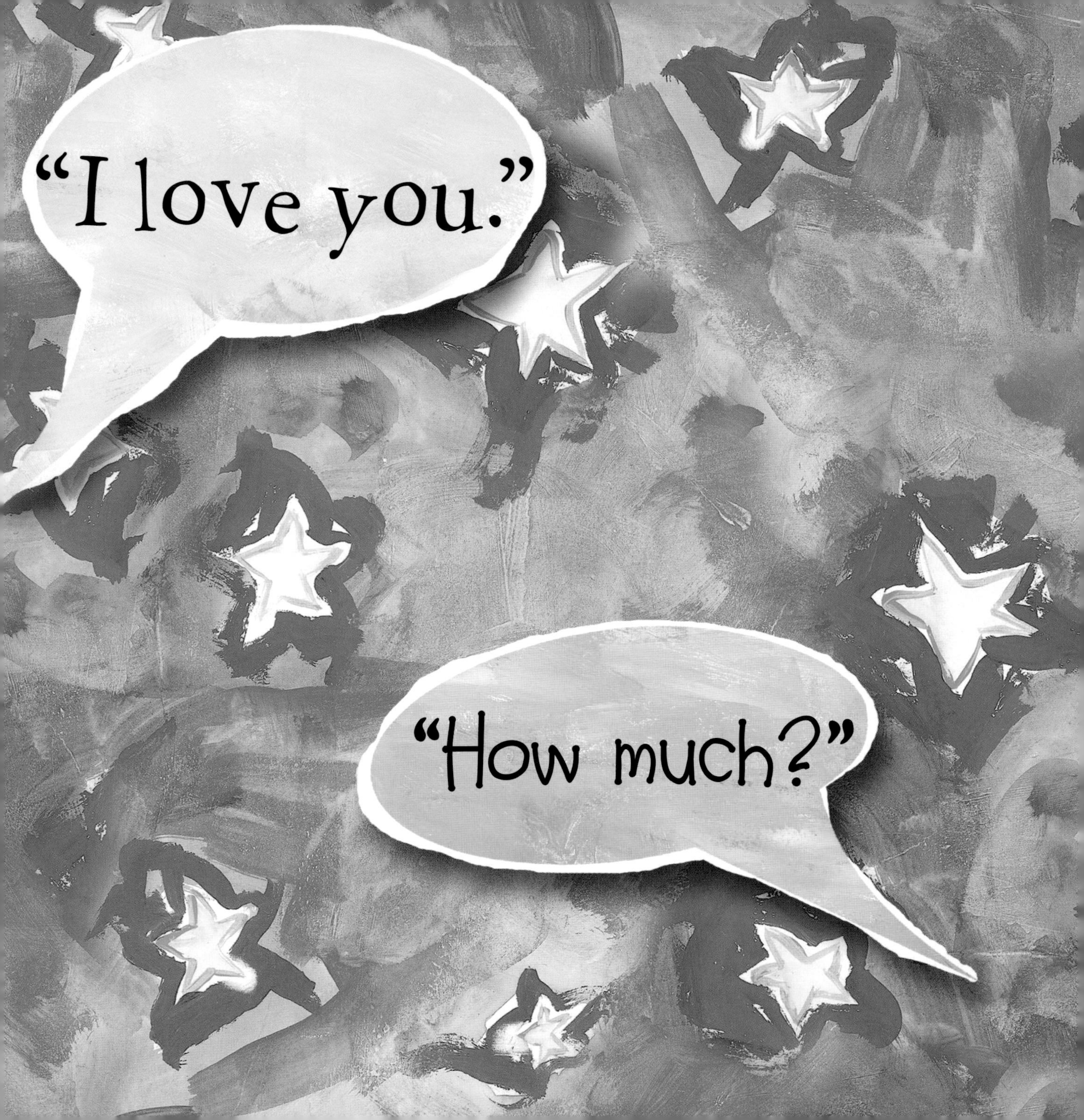
"I love you."
"How much?"

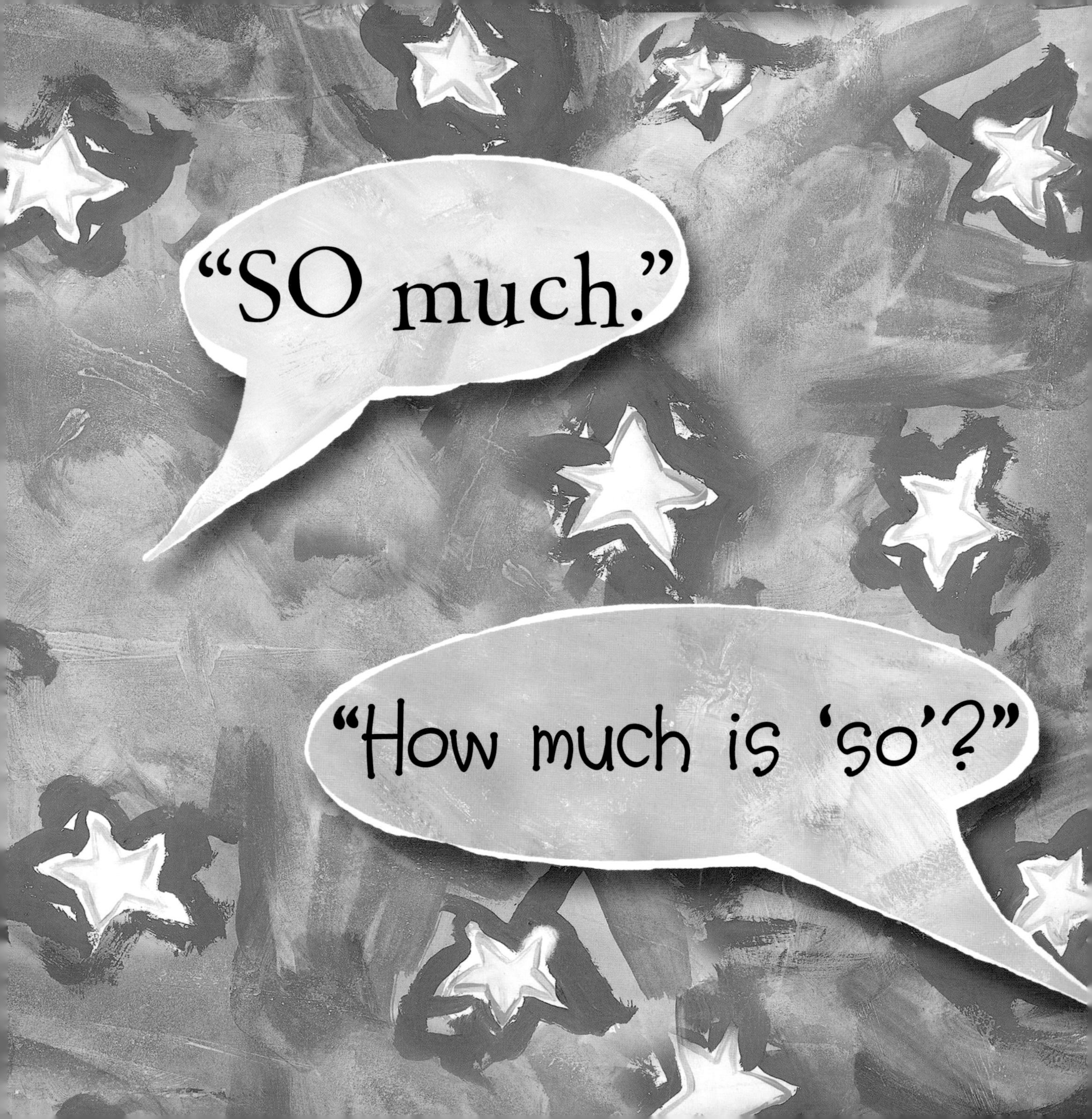
"SO much."
"How much is 'so'?"

"WAY, WAY MORE than you know…"